DRAGON MASTERS

SAVING THE SUN DRAGON

BY

TRACEY WEST

ILLUSTRATED BY

DAMIEN JONES

SCHOLASTIC INC.

DRAGON MASTERS

Read All the Books

TABLE OF CONTENTS

FOR MY FRIEND GEORGE,

who would make a good teacher of Dragon Masters. —TW

Special thanks to Damien Jones for his artistic contributions to this book.

Library of Congress Cataloging-in-Publication Data
West, Tracey, 1965- author.
Saving the sun dragon / by Tracey West ; illustrated by Graham Howells.
pages cm. — (Dragon masters ; 2)
Summary: The dark magic the dragons encountered in their first adventure has made Ana's sun dragon, Kepri, sick and Drake's earth dragon, Worm, teleports himself, Kepri, and the four young dragon masters far away from the castle in search of a cure—but the threat of the dark magic still remains.
ISBN 0-545-64625-1 (pbk. : alk. paper) — ISBN 0-545-64626-X (hardcover : alk. paper) — ISBN 0-545-64634-0 (ebook) 1. Dragons—Juvenile fiction. 2. Wizards—Juvenile fiction. 3. Magic—Juvenile fiction. [1. Dragons—Fiction. 2. Wizards—Fiction. 3. Magic—Fiction.] I. Howells, Graham, illustrator. II. Title.
PZ7.W51937Sav 2014
813.54—dc23
2013046257

ISBN 978-0-545-64626-0 (hardcover) / ISBN 978-0-545-64625-3 (paperback)

30 29 28 27 26 25 20 21 22 /0

Printed in China 62
First printing, December 2014
Edited by Katie Carella
Book design by Jessica Meltzer

CHAPTER 1

DRAGONS IN THE SKY

Drake shaded his eyes from the sun. He was standing in the Valley of Clouds behind King Roland's castle. Not long ago, Drake had never even been to the castle. But now he lived here, and he had an important job. He was a Dragon Master—someone who had been chosen by the Dragon Stone to work with dragons.

Above him, three dragons flew in the bright blue sky. Griffith, the wizard who taught the young Dragon Masters, watched as the dragons practiced flying.

Vulcan, a big, red Fire Dragon, flew across the valley. He shot a burst of fire into the air.

"Nice one!" yelled his Dragon Master, Rori. She had hair as red as Vulcan's flames.

Shu, a beautiful blue Water Dragon, didn't have wings. She glided through the air, riding the wind. Bo, her Dragon Master, watched her with a peaceful smile on his face.

The best flier was the yellow-and-white Sun Dragon, Kepri. She looped and swirled in the air. Then a rainbow streamed from her mouth. It arced across the sky. Kepri's Dragon Master, Ana, danced on the grass below her dragon. Her long, black hair swayed behind her.

Drake's dragon, Worm, was not like the other dragons. He was an Earth Dragon with a long, brown body. He couldn't fly. But Drake had just learned Worm could move things with the power of his mind. *What other amazing things can Worm do?* Drake wondered. He knew he had even more to learn about his dragon.

"It feels good to be outside, right, Worm?" Drake asked. The green Dragon Stone around Drake's neck tingled a bit. He smiled.

Each of the Dragon Masters wore a piece of the stone. It helped them connect with and train their dragons.

When the stone glowed, Drake knew that he and Worm had a very strong connection. Drake could sometimes hear Worm's voice inside his head when they were connecting. But the other Dragon Masters' stones had not glowed yet.

Drake looked back up at the sunny sky. Kepri's whole body shone with light.

Then Drake understood. "Oh, I get it. Kepri has light powers because she's a Sun Dragon, right?" Drake asked the other Dragon Masters.

Rori snorted. "Of course that's why. It's just like how Fire Dragons have fire powers, and Water Dragons have water powers."

Rori can be friendly sometimes, thought Drake. *And other times she's not friendly at all!*

His face turned red. "I'm still learning," he said. "I haven't been a Dragon Master as long as you."

Rori, Bo, and Ana had already been training for weeks when Drake got to the castle. He still felt like he had a lot of catching up to do.

Above them, Vulcan swooped down from the sky, showing off and shooting another stream of fire. It hit the ground right next to Griffith, and the grass burst into flames. The wizard jumped to the side.

"Careful there, Vulcan!" Griffith called out. He pointed his finger at the fire. Water flowed from his fingertip, and the flames went out.

Drake's eyes grew wide. "I will never get tired of seeing wizard magic," he said to Bo, who was standing beside him. Bo nodded.

Drake looked over at Worm. The dragon's eyes glowed bright green.

That's strange, thought Drake. *His eyes glow when he's using his powers. What could he be using his powers on right now?*

Worm was staring up at the sky.

Drake followed his gaze. Worm was looking at Kepri high up in the air. Her white wings had stopped flapping. Worm must have sensed that she was in trouble.

"Watch out! Kepri is falling!" Drake yelled.

CHAPTER 2
A SICK DRAGON

Ana looked up and started to scream. The other Dragon Masters also looked to the sky. Griffith pointed a finger at Kepri.

"I'll try to slow her down!" the wizard cried. Lightning sizzled from his finger. But before Griffith could use his magic, a red blur shot across the sky.

It was Vulcan, flying faster than Drake had ever seen him fly before. He lunged for Kepri and grabbed her with his front claws.

"Go, Vulcan!" Rori cheered.

Vulcan flew in a circle around the valley, slowing down. Then he gently placed Kepri in the grass.

Everyone ran to Kepri. The dragon's eyes were closed. Her breathing was loud and heavy. Ana stroked Kepri's head.

"Oh, Kepri, are you all right?" she asked, her voice shaking.

Griffith leaned over Kepri, frowning. "I'm afraid she doesn't look well," he said.

Ana turned to the wizard. "She has seemed a little off since last week—when the tunnel caved in. She gets tired easily. And sometimes her eyes look cloudy. I should have said something!"

Griffith put a hand on her shoulder. "It's not your fault, Ana," he said. "But are you sure Kepri only started looking sick *after* that night in the tunnel?"

Ana slowly nodded her head. "Yes. She was fine before then."

Drake, Bo, and Rori looked at one another. A week before, they had all tried to sneak out of the castle with their dragons. Since King Roland wanted to keep the dragons a secret, most dragon training had to take place underground. The Dragon Masters had only wanted to get outside to do some night flying.

Then a glowing red orb had flown into the tunnel that led to the valley.

The red ball of light scared Vulcan so he tried to get away.

His huge body banged into the tunnel walls, and he had made the tunnel cave in.

They were trapped.

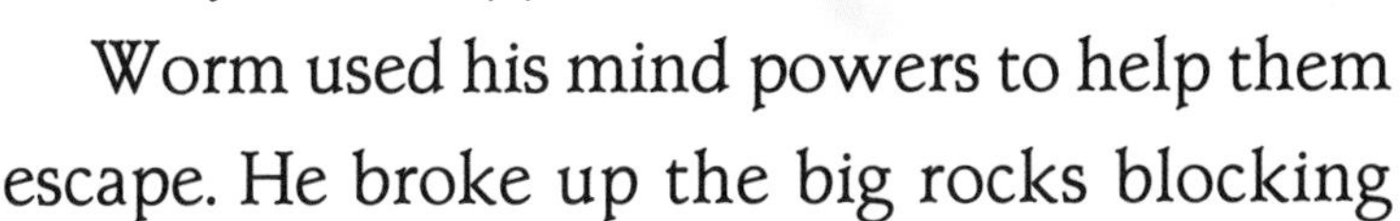

Worm used his mind powers to help them escape. He broke up the big rocks blocking the tunnel using only his thoughts. Worm had saved them all.

But now something was wrong with Kepri.

"Why did you ask about the cave-in, Griffith?" asked Bo.

"The red orb worries me," Griffith answered. "It must have been made by a dark wizard, as I had feared. And dark magic can make Sun Dragons sick."

"So Kepri's illness is connected to that weird ball?" asked Ana. "And the other dragons are okay because they're *not* Sun Dragons?"

"I think so," said Griffith.

"Do you *know* any dark wizards?" Drake asked with a shiver.

"No time for tales now," said Griffith with a wave of his hand.

Suddenly, Rori cried out. "Look! Kepri is getting up!"

The dragon had opened her eyes and was standing on all four legs.

"She looks well enough to walk back to the dragon caves," Griffith said. "Come along."

He led the Dragon Masters and their dragons back through the tunnel. The tunnel led to the big, underground Dragon Room. There, each dragon had a small cave.

When they got there, a big man with red hair waited for them. He wore a vest with a gold dragon on it, and a metal crown on his head. Two guards stood behind him.

Griffith stopped. "King Roland!" he said. "What brings you down here?"

The king frowned. "What is this I hear about a sick dragon?"

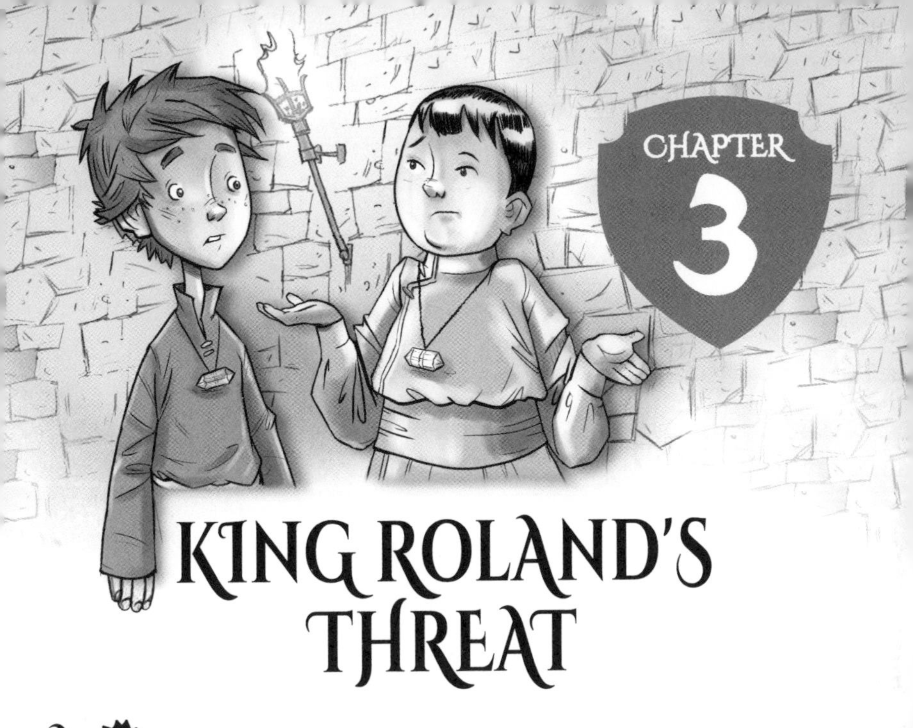

KING ROLAND'S THREAT

Drake looked over at his friend Bo. He could tell Bo was thinking the same thing he was: *How did the king know one of the dragons was sick?*

"I have spies hidden in the Valley of Clouds," the king said, as if he had read their minds. "You almost let these dragons escape once, Griffith. I want to make sure they are ready when I need them."

"I understand," Griffith said.

Drake remembered that when the tunnel had caved in, Griffith hadn't told the king that the Dragon Masters had taken the dragons out. Instead, he said the dragons had tried to escape. Griffith had lied to protect the Dragon Masters.

Griffith had only wanted to protect us when he told that lie, Drake thought. *But now the king is mad at* him *instead of* us*!*

"So I will ask you again, Griffith," said the king. "Is one of the dragons sick?"

"Yes, Your Majesty," said Griffith. "There seems to be something wrong with Kepri."

All eyes turned to Kepri. Her eyes were cloudy. And her long, graceful neck was drooping.

"First the dragons tried to escape, and now one is sick," said King Roland. "This makes me very unhappy, wizard. You are supposed to know all about dragons. Heal her!"

"I will look for a cure right away," Griffith promised.

"You had better find one soon," King Roland said, his eyes fixed on the wizard. "If not, I will find another wizard."

King Roland turned and stormed out of the caves. His guards followed.

Drake's stomach did a flip. *Another wizard? What would we do without Griffith?*

"What do we do now?" Ana asked Griffith, stroking Kepri's head.

"I have many books about dragons," the wizard replied. "We will start there."

"*We?* You mean we can help?" Drake asked.

"Of course!" Griffith said. "Please take your dragons into their caves. Then meet me in the Training Room. We must act quickly to save Kepri!"

THE WIZARD'S POTION

The Dragon Masters dropped off their dragons and headed to the Training Room. The section where Griffith taught lessons was kind of like a cave.

Most days, everyone wanted to be outside in the Valley of Clouds. Drake loved it there because it reminded him of working in his family's onion fields. But today, nobody was complaining about staying inside. Everyone wanted to help Kepri.

When they walked into the classroom, they saw a giant pile of books on the table.

"Everyone take a book," Griffith said, pointing to a stack of books. "A dark wizard made that orb. So we must find a cure for Sun Dragons who have been touched by dark magic. Quickly, now!" He was already flipping through *All About Sun Dragons.*

Drake took *Dragons 101* back to his desk. The room was quiet, except for the sound of turning pages. Drake read and read, but couldn't find anything. No one could.

Then Rori held up *Dragon Lore.* "I found something!" she cried. "Listen: 'Each Sun Dragon is born with a Moon Dragon twin. These twins can cure each other of almost anything.' Is this true? Does Kepri have a Moon Dragon twin?"

Griffith frowned. "I do not know. And if she does have a twin, that twin is likely very far away from here. There's no way we could find the Moon Dragon in time."

Ana stood up. "Well, my book has a potion in it called Wicked-Away," she said. "It heals creatures harmed by dark magic."

She brought the book to Griffith. His eyes lit up.

"This might do it! It's not just for Sun Dragons so I'm not sure if it will work. But it's worth a try," he said. "Drake and Bo, go to my workshop. Bring back a jar of moonbeams and a sack of sunflower seeds. Hurry!"

The boys raced into the hall to Griffith's workshop. The workshop was filled with bottles and jars. The bottles and jars were stuffed with strange plants and filled with potions.

Drake walked to the left side of the room, and Bo took the right side. Drake picked up a jar with purple liquid inside.

"Lily dew," he read out loud. He checked a few more jars—and then saw something glowing on the top shelf. Standing on his toes, he grabbed it.

A pale blue light shimmered inside the jar. Drake read the label.

"Moonbeams! I've got them!" he shouted.

"And I've got the seeds," Bo said. "Let's go!"

When they got back to the classroom, Rori was stirring liquid in a black metal pot. Ana was reading directions aloud from her book. Griffith clapped his hands when he saw the two boys.

"That was fast! Now, let's make this healing potion," said Griffith. "Drake, empty the jar into the pot. Bo, add three seeds, please."

Drake carefully opened the jar lid. The moonbeams slid out like water. Then Bo dropped in three black seeds.

"Keep stirring, Rori," Griffith said.

Rori stirred. The liquid turned blue and started to shine. A soft light came from the pot. Griffith scooped up some liquid with a ladle and put it in a clean jar.

"Will this potion make Kepri feel better?" Bo asked.

"There's only one way to find out," Griffith said.

They all walked to Kepri's cave. Her eyes were closed, and her yellow scales had lost their shine.

Griffith handed the jar to Ana. "You are her Dragon Master. She will listen to you. She must drink this," he said.

Ana nodded. She walked up to Kepri. "I have something for you," she said softly.

Kepri opened her eyes. She smiled when she saw Ana. "We made it for you—to make you well again," Ana said, holding up the jar.

Kepri opened her mouth. Ana slowly poured the potion inside.

"This has got to work," she whispered.

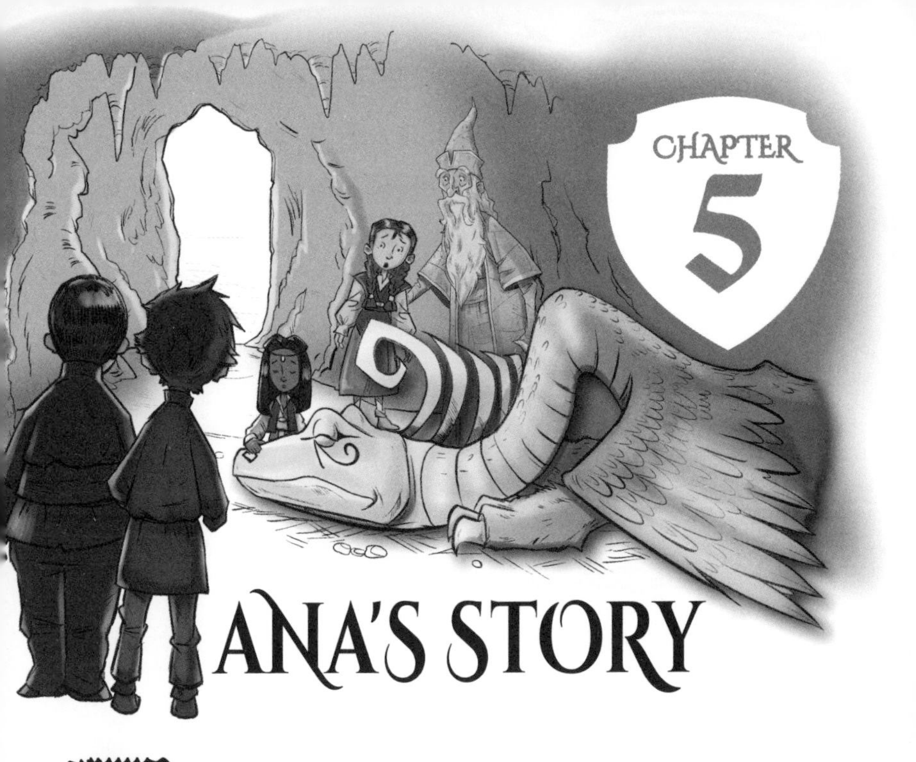

ANA'S STORY

The Dragon Masters crowded around Kepri.

"Feel better?" Ana asked her dragon. But Kepri just closed her eyes again.

Bo looked at Griffith. "Will the potion work right away?"

"I do not know," Griffith said. "We must wait and see. You all should head to dinner while I stay with Kepri."

"I'm not leaving her," Ana said firmly.

Griffith put a gentle hand on her shoulder. "Ana, you must take care of yourself," he said. "You must stay strong for Kepri. I will send for you if anything changes."

The Dragon Masters left the cave, leaving a worried wizard and a sick dragon behind them.

Up in the dining room, they all picked at their dinner. Ana only ate a few bites of food. Drake ate some carrots and chicken—but only about half as much as usual. Bo stared at his plate. Even Rori was quiet for a change.

Then the door at the end of the room banged open. One of the king's soldiers walked in.

"Do you have news about Kepri?" Ana asked.

The soldier walked over to Drake without saying a word. He handed him a rolled-up piece of paper.

Drake opened it. "It's a letter from my mom!"

Dear Drake,

It is good here in the fields. The onions are big.

I know you are busy helping the king with his special project. But I miss you. Work hard!

Love

Your Mother

Drake felt tears sting his eyes. He knew he was doing important work for the king, but he still missed his mom.

"I wish I could tell my family about the dragons," Drake said.

"They have to be kept a secret," Rori warned.

"I wish my father would write to me more often," Ana said. "I'd like to hear about his adventures."

"What kind of adventures?" Bo asked.

"My father sells beautiful fabrics," she said. "He travels all over far-away lands selling them. And we lived near the pyramids, so I often went there with him."

"What's a pyramid?" Rori asked.

"It holds a king's body after he dies. It's sort of shaped like this." Ana made a triangle shape with her hands. "The pyramids are bigger than anything you've ever seen."

"Your dad's adventures sound amazing," said Drake.

"They are." Ana sighed. "But they're also dangerous. There are many robbers on the roads. The robbers steal from people who have goods to sell—like our fabrics. And they often steal gold and other treasures from the pyramids. That is why my father did not argue when King Roland's men came for me. He knew I would be safer elsewhere."

Ana looked sad. Bo was quiet.

I guess everyone else is just as homesick as I am, Drake thought.

After dinner, Drake and Bo went to the room that they shared. Drake climbed into bed and fell asleep right away. He dreamed of rivers and big tombs shaped like triangles. Then the desert sky turned green . . . bright green. Drake woke up.

The green Dragon Stone around his neck was glowing brightly.

Worm needs me! Drake thought.

Then he heard Worm's voice inside his mind.

Come now!

WORM CALLS

Drake jumped out of bed. He shook Bo awake.

"Worm needs us!" Drake cried.

That was all Bo needed to hear. The boys raced downstairs to the door that led to the dragon training area. Drake tried to open it.

"It's locked!" Drake cried.

"Good thing I have a key," said a voice.

Drake and Bo turned around. Rori and Ana were standing there. Rori held up a key.

"Where did you get that?" Drake asked.

"I swiped it from one of the castle guards when I first got here," Rori said. "It's a skeleton key. It opens up *all* the locks in the castle."

"We came running as soon as we heard you two stomping down the hall!" Ana added. "We figured something was up."

"I'm glad you came. But please hurry!" Drake said.

Rori opened the door.

When they got to Kepri's cave, Worm was in front of it.

How did Worm get out of his cave? Drake wondered.

"Worm, what's wrong?" he asked.

Worm nodded toward Kepri. The gate to her cave was open and the Dragon Masters stepped inside. Griffith was asleep in the corner. Books were piled around him.

Kepri was asleep, too—but she looked sicker than before. Her scales looked dull. She looked thin and pale. Her breathing was loud and heavy.

The Dragon Masters were stunned.

"She wasn't this sick earlier," Rori said. "Did the potion make her worse?"

"Maybe it just didn't work," Bo said.

"We have to *do something*!" Ana cried.

Drake looked at Worm.

"Isn't there anything we can do?" Drake whispered.

Worm's body began to glow. Drake wasn't sure why, but he knew just what to do. He put one hand on Worm's snout and one hand on Kepri's tail.

"Everybody, touch Worm! Now!" he yelled.

Startled, his friends obeyed. They all laid their hands on Worm.

Griffith's eyes snapped open.

"What is going on?" the wizard asked.

But before Drake could answer, green light exploded in the room, blinding them.

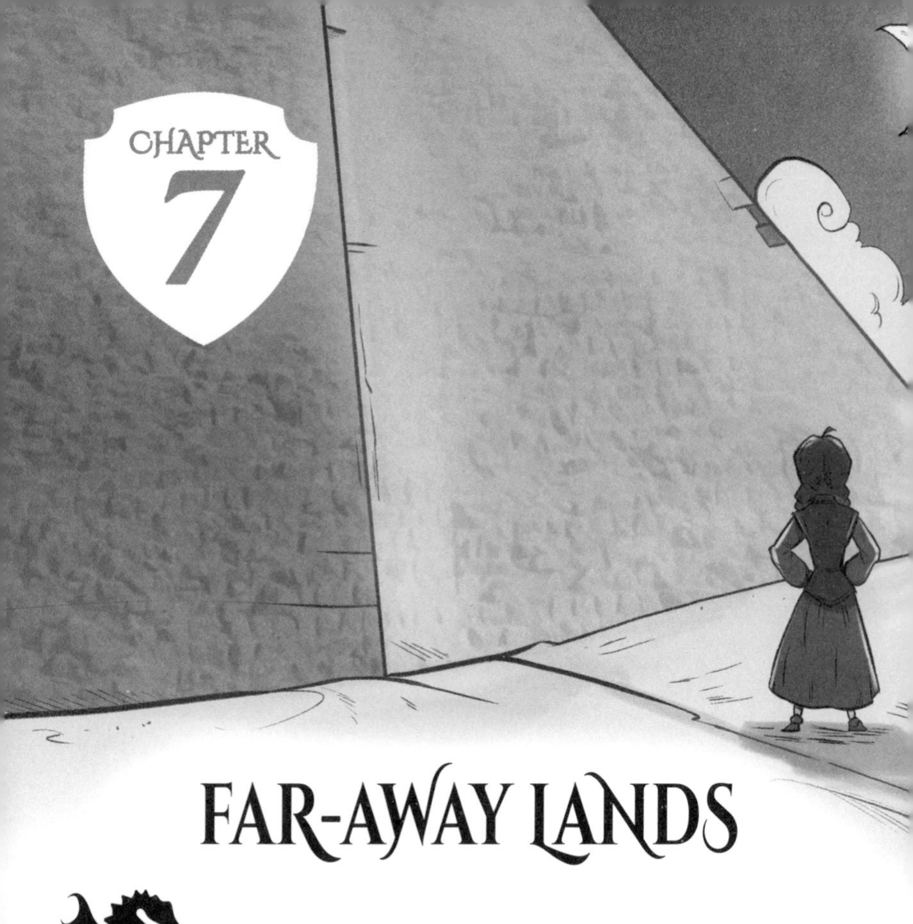

CHAPTER 7

FAR-AWAY LANDS

Drake felt weird. He couldn't feel the ground under his feet. But he could still feel his hand on Worm. His stomach did a flip-flop.

Then the green light faded. Drake blinked. His feet landed on sand, and he could feel cool air on his face.

Worm, Kepri, and the Dragon Masters were standing on a pathway. A white stone wall lined one side of the path. On the other side of them was a tall, strangely shaped building. Griffith was not with them.

Worm, why did you bring us here? Drake wondered.

Drake looked up at the big building. Each of the building's four sides was shaped like a triangle. The pointy top was capped with shining gold.

Ana's eyes got wide. "A pyramid!" she cried.

"Drake, what have you done? Where are we?" Rori asked. She sounded scared.

Ana turned to her. "I think we are in my homeland."

"But how . . . ?" Drake started to say. Then he looked at Worm. The dragon's green eyes were shining. "Worm must have used his mind powers to bring us here!"

"That's impossible!" said Rori. "Dragons can't travel halfway across the world using their minds."

"Look around you, Rori," Bo said. "It must be possible. We are no longer in the Kingdom of Bracken."

"But why didn't Worm bring Vulcan and Shu with us?" Rori asked.

Drake thought back to Kepri's cave. "We were all touching Worm. And I was touching Kepri. But the other dragons were still in their caves."

"And now we are here, in the land where Kepri and I were born," said Ana.

"Wait! Remember what I read in Griffith's book—about Sun Dragon twins?" Rori asked, her voice getting excited. "It said that every Sun Dragon has a Moon Dragon twin that can heal it."

"So Kepri's twin might be here!" said Bo.

"Do you think that's why Worm brought us here?" asked Drake.

Suddenly, they heard loud voices. The voices came from the other side of the stone wall. Drake didn't understand the language.

But Ana did. "Oh, no! Robbers! They often come to the pyramids to steal things. That must be why they are here! We cannot let anyone see us—or our dragons!"

"But there's nowhere to hide!" said Bo.

Just then, a boy stepped out from the shadows. He had golden-brown skin and black hair, like Ana.

"Follow me!" he said.

A STRANGE BOY

Rori stepped closer to the boy. "Why should we follow you?" she asked. "We don't even know you!"

"Trust me," the boy said, just as the robbers' voices grew louder. "I am surprised to see that you have dragons. But I know how to keep them safe. Come on!"

"We must hurry!" Ana said.

They had no choice. The boy waved for them to follow him. He touched the pyramid. One of the big stones pushed in, revealing an opening.

A secret door! Drake thought.

"Inside, quick!" the boy said. "Dragons first."

He stepped aside to let them in. Kepri was weak, but Worm nudged her gently with his nose. She stepped through the door. As Drake walked past the boy, he saw a cord around the boy's neck. Something green and sparkling was dangling from the cord.

A Dragon Stone!

The boy slipped in behind Drake and the secret door closed. They were inside a dark tunnel. Flaming torches lined the walls.

Drake turned to the boy.

"Who are you? Are you a Dragon Master, too?" He pointed to the green stone around the boy's neck. Ana, Rori, and Bo gasped when they saw it.

The boy smiled. "My name is Heru," he said. "I do not know what a Dragon Master is. My father gave me this stone."

"King Roland calls us Dragon Masters," Drake explained. "We were chosen by the Dragon Stone to work with dragons."

"I have not heard of King Roland. Are you from far away?" Heru asked.

Bo nodded. "Very far."

Heru frowned. "How strange. Can you tell me why Wati brought me here tonight?"

Ana was stroking Kepri's neck. The dragon's eyes seemed brighter now that she was inside the pyramid.

"Who's Wati?" Drake asked.

Heru grinned. "He is my dragon."

By now they had left the tunnel. They were inside a dark room. Drake looked up. The ceiling was so far above that he couldn't see it. Then something appeared out of the darkness. A huge, black dragon flew down from the ceiling. His eyes glowed bright yellow.

"*Aaaiieeeee!*"

With a loud cry, the dragon flew down, charging right at them!

KEPRI AND WATI

"Get down, everyone!" Drake yelled. The Dragon Masters all ducked. But the dragon was not after them.

He came to a stop right next to Kepri. The dragon wrapped his wings around her and made a happy, purring sound.

"It looks like they know each other," Drake said, pointing to the two dragons.

Wati was gently stroking Kepri's back with one of his wings. Her eyes were closed, and her head was drooping. Wati had black scales, and Kepri had white scales. But they had the same graceful bodies and yellow-tipped wings.

"They look a lot alike," said Bo.

"Yes, except that Kepri has light scales and Wati has dark scales," added Drake. "Light and dark—"

"Like the sun and the moon!" Rori yelled.

Ana's mouth dropped open. "This is what we'd been hoping for!"

Heru looked thrilled. "Wati is a Moon Dragon. My father taught me that all Moon Dragons have a twin—a Sun Dragon," he said. "Wati must have known that Kepri would be in this pyramid tonight. That explains why he suddenly flew off earlier. I am glad that I followed him here."

Drake was starting to figure it out. "So, Kepri must have known that Wati could heal her," he said. "And she must have told Worm about her twin. That's how Worm knew to bring her here!"

"Is Worm an Earth Dragon?" Heru asked.

Drake nodded.

"They have amazing powers," said Heru. "Worm did the right thing when he brought Kepri here."

Rori gave Drake a high five. Ana hugged Worm. "Thank you, Worm!"

Then Bo looked nervously at Kepri and Wati. "Look!"

Wati was standing up on his hind legs with his wings spread out wide.

"Everyone, step back, quick!" Heru yelled.

They moved away just as Wati opened his mouth. A ribbon of dark colors streamed out.

It looks almost like a rainbow, Drake thought, *except it's all blue and black and purple.*

Wati's rainbow ribbon grew and grew. It swirled around Kepri's body. She stirred a little, but her eyes were still closed.

Ana squeezed Drake's hand.

The light from the blue-and-purple rainbow grew bigger and shone brighter. The Dragon Masters had to shield their eyes.

Then . . . *whoosh*! The light swirled all around them.

ROBBERS!

The light began to fade. Drake blinked. Everyone looked at Kepri. Her white scales looked shiny again. Her eyes were open and clear. She did not look sick anymore, just a little tired.

"Kepri!" Ana cried happily. She started to run to her when—

Bam! They heard the sound of wood breaking. Loud voices were coming from the tunnel that led to the hidden chamber.

"The robbers are coming!" Ana yelled. "We must get out of here!"

Rori balled her hands into fists. "We'll fight them!" she growled.

Kepri and Wati roared as four men dressed in black ran into the chamber. They carried bows and arrows, spears, and clubs.

When the robbers saw the dragons, they stopped, their eyes wide. Then one of the men started yelling to the others. The men raised their weapons and took aim at the dragons.

"They want to capture the dragons!" Ana warned.

Wati quickly sprang into action. He shot a black beam of light from his mouth. The beam hit the first robber in the chest and knocked him down.

Drake's heart pounded. He moved closer to Worm.

Then the second robber stepped forward. He sent an arrow flying right at Kepri.

"No!" Ana cried. Then she jumped in the path of the arrow!

CHAPTER 11

FLYING

Drake watched in horror as the arrow flew toward Ana. He dove toward her, hoping to knock her out of the way. But before he could reach her, the arrow stopped in midair—inches from Ana's face.

Drake landed with a thud. He picked himself up and looked at Worm. The dragon's green eyes were glowing. Drake knew what that meant: Worm had used his mind powers to stop the arrow.

The arrow fell to the floor. And Worm wasn't finished! Next the weapons flew from the hands of the robbers. They slammed into the wall, breaking into pieces.

The four robbers floated up off the floor. Their legs dangled beneath them. They shouted at Worm.

Drake could see the green light in Worm's eyes starting to flicker.

"Worm can't hold them up there much longer," he guessed. "We must get out of here!"

"Get on the dragons!" Heru yelled.

Heru and Rori climbed onto Wati. Ana climbed onto Kepri's back. Drake and Bo climbed onto Worm.

"Wati! Blast the top of the pyramid!" Heru ordered.

Wati aimed a black beam of light at the top of the chamber. A bright rainbow ribbon came from Kepri's mouth and joined it. The top of the pyramid opened up!

"Now we fly out," Heru said. "Go!"

Wati flew up, and Kepri flew up behind him. Worm stayed on the ground. The light in his eyes kept flickering. The robbers' feet were almost touching the floor now.

Drake saw that Worm couldn't use his power to do too many things at once. He knew his dragon couldn't fly like the other dragons. But Worm could take them somewhere else in a flash—if he was strong enough.

"Worm, get us out of here!" Drake yelled.

Worm let go of his grip on the robbers. They tumbled to the floor. Then they quickly got up, angrily charging toward Drake, Bo, and Worm. The dragon's eyes glowed green.

"Hold on tight, Bo!" Drake yelled.

One second, they were in the chamber. The next, they were outside the pyramid!

CHAPTER 12

ANA'S DECISION

Drake and Bo climbed off Worm's back. They looked up. The sun was just starting to rise. Kepri and Wati were flying around.

"We can't stay here long," Bo said. "Soon the villagers will wake up, and we can't let them see the dragons."

Drake nodded. "Yes, and Griffith is probably worried about us."

Kepri and Wati glided down and landed next to them. Ana, Heru, and Rori climbed off the dragons' backs. They ran over to Drake and Bo.

"You made it!" Ana cried.

"We figured that Worm could do his cool Earth-Dragon-thing and get you out of there in a blink," Rori said.

Drake smiled at Worm. "Yeah, he's awesome."

Then the twin dragons flew up again and circled the golden top of the pyramid.

"Kepri and Wati look so happy together," Bo said.

Ana sighed. "I am so glad Kepri is better," she said. "It's all because of Wati. He knew how to heal her when no one else could. I really think she should stay here with him." She sounded sad.

"But she's *your* dragon," Drake said. "She should stay with *you*."

Ana shook her head. "I don't have a strong connection with Kepri. Not like the one that you have with Worm. Your stone glows when you and Worm connect—just like earlier tonight when he called to you. My Dragon Stone has never glowed."

"But Griffith said it would happen to you, too," Drake said. He looked at Bo and Rori. "To all of you."

Ana had tears in her eyes. "I might never know now. It seems like Kepri is better off without me."

Heru put a hand on her shoulder. "Listen to Drake, Ana. I knew Wati for a year before my stone glowed," he said. "It takes patience."

Drake turned to Heru. "You said you weren't a Dragon Master. But you have a Dragon Stone and your own dragon. How are you *not* a Dragon Master?"

Heru shrugged. "It is *your* king who has called you a Dragon Master. I serve no king. All I know is that for many ages, my family has served dragons. When dragons come to us, we help them."

King Roland doesn't want to help dragons, Drake thought. *He just wants us to train them.*

"We must get back to our kingdom," Bo said. "The castle will be waking up soon. If King Roland finds the dragons missing . . ."

Drake shuddered. "That would be bad for us—and for Griffith!"

He turned to Ana. "We must go. Do you want to see if Kepri will come with us?"

"I've decided that she should stay with Wati," Ana said sadly. "I will say good-bye. Let me call her."

CHAPTER 13

ONE LAST GOOD-BYE

"Wait!" Drake yelled. He saw something: the Dragon Stone on Ana's neck. It was glowing! Drake pointed to it. Bo, Rori, and Heru all turned to look.

"Ana, your stone!" they cried.

Ana gazed down at the glowing stone. She got a strange look in her eyes.

"Ana, what is it?" Rori asked.

"I think I can hear Kepri's voice . . . inside my head!" Ana said.

Everyone was quiet as Ana listened. She got a smile on her face. She looked up at Kepri flying in the sky.

"Kepri wants to come back to be with her brother one day," Ana said. "Just like I want to come back to my family. But until then, she wants to stay with me in the kingdom of Bracken."

"I'm so happy for you," said Drake.

"Yes. We would all miss Kepri as much as you," added Rori.

The sun was higher in the sky now.

"Ana, we must go," said Bo softly. "Everyone, including our king, will be waking up soon."

Ana nodded. "Come, Kepri," she called out.

Kepri and Wati circled the pyramid one last time. Then both dragons swooped down. They landed next to Worm and the Dragon Masters.

Drake smiled at Heru. "Thank you for helping us," he said.

Heru smiled. "No problem. Perhaps we will meet again."

"That would be nice," Drake said. He turned to his friends. "Okay, everyone. Just like last time. Place one hand on Worm."

Ana hugged Wati. Her cheeks were shiny with tears as she broke away. Then she put one hand on Kepri and one hand on Worm.

"Okay, Worm," Drake said. "Home, please."

Worm's body started to glow green once more . . .

CHAPTER 14

HOME

A few seconds later, the Dragon Masters were all back in the Training Room in King Roland's castle.

"Good heavens!" a voice cried.

When Worm's light faded, Drake saw Griffith standing in front of them—with another wizard! Like Griffith, he had a white beard. But he was a head shorter than Griffith and twice as round.

Griffith looked at Kepri. "My goodness! She is cured!" he said. "When I saw Worm glow green and you all vanished, I trusted that Worm would know where to find a cure."

"Yes! Worm took us to meet Kepri's twin, a Moon Dragon named Wati," Drake explained. "Wati cured her."

"Just like it said in *Dragon Lore*!" Rori added.

Griffith put his hands together. "Wonderful!" he cried. "Worm, you are full of surprises."

"He is very unusual," said the shorter wizard, stepping up close to Worm.

"Dragon Masters, meet Diego," Griffith said, pointing to the wizard.

"Very nice to meet you," Diego said.

"I have asked Diego for his help," Griffith said. "We have been trying to find out which dark wizard could have sent that red orb."

"I know only one wizard with a heart evil enough for this type of dark magic," Diego said. "His name is Maldred."

Drake shivered. "Why would Maldred send the orb here?"

"That's something we still have to figure out," Griffith said.

Diego put an arm on Griffith's shoulder. "Together."

Everyone was quiet as they thought about this. Then the loud voice of a castle guard broke the silence.

"All rise for King Roland!"

Diego snapped his fingers and vanished in a puff of smoke. Then the king stomped in with two guards behind him.

"Did you heal my dragon, wizard?" King Roland asked.

Drake thought quickly. If the king found out that Worm had taken them far away, he might get mad. Or he might try to use Worm's special power. *What if he takes Worm away from me?*

"Griffith made a potion, and it worked," Drake lied. He pointed to Kepri. "See?"

"I didn't ask you, boy," King Roland said crossly.

But the king's frown faded when he saw Kepri. "Hmm. I see it's true. Good work, wizard. It looks like I won't have to replace you with another wizard . . . for now."

Then the king and his guards turned and left.

Griffith smiled at Drake. "Thank you," he said.

"Will you tell the king about that dark wizard named Maldred?" Bo asked.

"There is not much his army can do against Maldred's dark magic," Griffith said. "It will be up to us to protect this kingdom."

Rori snorted. "Vulcan won't be afraid of some old wizard."

"And Vulcan won't be fighting that wizard alone," Ana said, looking at Kepri. "All of us will help."

Drake looked at Worm. He was proud of how his dragon had helped Kepri. "Yes," he said, turning to his friends. "Whatever happens, we're all in this together!"

TRACEY WEST likes the sun because it helps her garden grow. But on hot summer days, she loves being outside at night under the moonlight. That's how she knew that Kepri the Sun Dragon would need to have a Moon Dragon twin!

Tracey has written dozens of books for kids. She does her writing in the house she shares with her husband and three stepkids. She also has plenty of animal friends to keep her company. She has two dogs, seven chickens, and one cat, who sits on her desk when she writes! Thankfully, the cat does not weigh as much as a dragon.

GRAHAM HOWELLS lives with his wife and two sons in west Wales, a place full of castles, and legends of wizards and dragons.

There are many stories about the dragons of Wales. One story tells of a large, legless dragon—sort of like Worm! Graham's home is also near where Merlin the great wizard is said to lie asleep in a crystal cave.

Graham has illustrated several books. He has created artwork for film, television, and board games, too. Graham also writes stories for children. In 2009, he won the Tir Na N'Og award for *Merlin's Magical Creatures*.

DRAGON MASTERS

SAVING THE SUN DRAGON

Questions and Activities

Name some similarities between the Dragon Masters and their dragons. For example, how is Bo similar to Shu?

What CAUSES Kepri to get sick?

Who are Heru and Wati? Why are they important?

Why does Drake LIE to King Roland on page 88?

Do you think Kepri belongs with Ana or with Wati? Why? Write about your opinion.